Daisy
1 2 3

Peter Catalanotto

A RICHARD JACKSON BOOK
ATHENEUM BOOKS FOR YOUNG READERS
New York   London   Toronto   Sydney   Singapore

For P. S. 128

Atheneum Books for Young Readers
An imprint of Simon & Schuster Children's Publishing Division
1230 Avenue of the Americas
New York, New York 10020
Copyright © 2003 by Peter Catalanotto
All rights reserved, including the right of reproduction in whole or in part in any form.
The text of this book is set in Fink Roman and Stovetop.
The illustrations are rendered in watercolor.
Manufactured in China
First Edition
2 4 6 8 10 9 7 5 3 1
Library of Congress Cataloging-in-Publication Data
Catalanotto, Peter.
Daisy 1, 2, 3 / Peter Catalanotto.
p.   cm.
"A Richard Jackson book."
Summary: Mrs. Tuttle teaches a dog obedience class to twenty Dalmatians who are all named
Daisy, but each one has some feature that makes her easily identifiable.
ISBN 0-689-85457-9
[1. Dalmatian dog—Juvenile fiction. 2. Dalmatian dog—Fiction. 3. Dogs—Fiction. 4. Counting.]
I. Title. II. Title: Daisy one, two, three.
PZ7 .C26878 Dai 2003
[E]—dc21   2002010716

Mrs. Tuttle has twenty Dalmatians
in her Saturday morning obedience class.
They are all named Daisy.

Her assistant, Doris,
wonders how Mrs. Tuttle tells them apart.

Mrs. Tuttle
finds it quite simple.

Daisy **1** has one peculiar spot.

Daisy 2 wears two name tags.

2

Daisy 4...

. . . does four tricks.

Daisy **6** adopted six parakeets.

6

Daisy 8 fetches eight slippers at a time.

Daisy **9** hired
nine security guards.

9

Daisy 10 knows ten dance steps.

Daisy 11 will not share
any of her eleven chew toys.

11

Daisy **12** needs to be home
by twelve, midnight.

12

Daisy 13 works as a tour guide
for thirteen hamsters.

13

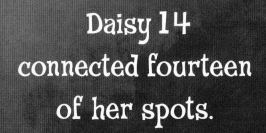

Daisy 14
connected fourteen
of her spots.

14

Daisy **15** can hear squirrels
fifteen miles away.

Daisy **16** has sixteen favorite collars.

16

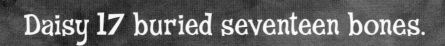

Daisy **17** buried seventeen bones.

Daisy 18 is quite proud
of her eighteen toenails.

18

Daisy 19
sports nineteen
impressive
spots.

19

Daisy 20
fools twenty fleas.

20

"Oh, I see," says Doris.
"Each dog has her place."

"Yes," says Mrs. Tuttle.
"They all have their spots."